JAMES STEVENSON

A VILLAGE FULL OF VALENTINES

GREENWILLOW BOOKS NEW YORK

For Josie

Watercolor paints and a black pen were used for the full-color art.
The text type is Leawood.

Printed in Hong Kong

The Library of Congress has cataloged the
Greenwillow Books edition of *A Village Full of
Valentines* as follows:

Stevenson, James (date)
A village full of valentines / by James Stevenson.
p.   cm.
Summary: Each animal who lives in a little village
celebrates Valentine's Day in a different way.
ISBN 0-688-13602-8 (trade)
ISBN 0-688-13603-6 (lib. bdg.)
[1. Valentines—Fiction.
2. Valentine's Day—Fiction.]
I. Title.   PZ7.S84748Vi   1995
[E]—dc20   94-624   CIP   AC

5 7 9 10 8 6 4
First Mulberry edition, 1998
ISBN 0-688-15839-0

CONTENTS

.1.
CLIFFORD'S RULE

"Sending any valentines this year, Clifford?"
asked Maureen.

"Certainly not!" said Clifford.

"Why not?" said Maureen.

"I have a strict rule," said Clifford.
"I never send a valentine to anybody
 unless they send me one first."
"You might have to wait a while,"
 said Maureen.
"I already have," said Clifford.
"How long?" said Maureen.
"Fifty-six years," said Clifford.

.2.
MONA, TINA, AND MARY LOU

"I have an idea," said Mona.

"What is it?" said Tina.

"Let's hear it," said Mary Lou.

"Why don't we make valentines together this year?" said Mona.

"Great idea!" said Tina. "It will save time."
"And we'll have fun working together!"
 said Mary Lou.
"I'll cut out the hearts with scissors,"
 said Mona.

"I'll paste on the frilly stuff," said Tina.

"What will I do?" said Mary Lou.
"You can address envelopes,"
 said Mona.
"Wait a minute," said Mary Lou.
"That's no fun."

"Okay," said Tina. "You can lick stamps."
"Stamps are icky!" said Mary Lou.
"Why don't *you* lick stamps?"

"All right, all right," said Mona. "You can
crayon little flowers and hearts and
things on the envelopes. How's that?"
"I don't want to do envelopes," said
Mary Lou. "I want to do the insides!"
"*We're* doing insides," said Tina.
"I want to use scissors," said Mary Lou.
"I had scissors first," said Mona.
"I want to use paste," said Mary Lou.

"Wait," said Mona. "I have an idea."

"What is it?" said Tina.

"Let's all do our own valentines," said Mona.

"Fine," said Tina. "Then we can surprise
 each other."

"And we can still be friends," said Mary Lou.

They all went home and got to work.

.3.
DONALD'S SPECIAL VALENTINE

"Here's your valentine, you lucky bird," said Donald to Tricia. "Where's mine?"

"This looks a lot like that valentine Barbara
  gave you last year," said Tricia.
"Does it?" said Donald.
"A lot," said Tricia. "And wrinkled, too."
"You could smooth it out," said Donald.
"Thanks," said Tricia.

"So where's mine?" said Donald.

"I'm kind of in a hurry."

"Shut your eyes and put out your hand,"
said Tricia.

"This better be special," said Donald.

"It is," said Tricia.

Donald shut his eyes and put out his hand.

"There!" said Tricia. "Happy Valentine's Day!"
Donald opened his eyes. "Where is it?"
he said.

"In your hand," said Tricia. "The world's
tiniest valentine! Do you like it?"
"How can I tell?" said Donald.

"Hold it very carefully so it doesn't
  blow away," said Tricia.
"Like this?" said Donald. He cupped
  his hands.
"Exactly!" said Tricia. "Make sure
  you don't lose it."

"Can I show it to other people?"
 asked Donald.
"You could give them a quick look,"
 said Tricia, "if you're careful."
 Donald walked away.
"Who wants to see my tiny valentine?"
 he called.

.4.
THE MOST BEAUTIFUL VALENTINE EVER MADE

David was walking past Murray's house when he heard groaning and moaning from inside. David knocked on the door. "It's me," he said. "Is that you groaning and moaning, Murray?"

"Yes, David, it is," said Murray.
"I'm very miserable."

David went in. "Still working on your valentine for Beatrice?" he said.

"Yes," said Murray with a moan. "This is the third day, and I'm getting nowhere." The floor was heaped with red paper hearts. Murray looked worn out.

"What's the problem?" asked David.

"I want to give Beatrice the most beautiful valentine ever made," said Murray. "And it's not easy."

He began cutting another heart from a new sheet of red paper.

David looked at the piles of hearts on the floor. Some were shaped like this 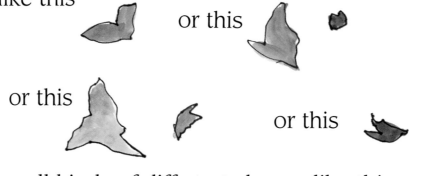 or this

or this

or this

or all kinds of different shapes like this.

"How does this one look?" said Murray,
  holding his newest heart up to the light.

"It's a little fatter on one side than the other,"
  said David. Murray began snipping.
"Not that side," said David. "The other side."
  Murray snipped the other side.
"Now is it okay?" he said.
"Well, it looks kind of skinny," said David.
"Skinny and sad."

Murray groaned. He crumpled up the heart and threw it on the floor. "I may have to give up," he said. "The most beautiful valentine ever made is just too hard." He sat down. "Of course it is," said David. "Why don't you make the *second* most beautiful valentine ever made?"

"That would be a lot easier," said Murray.

"Or the *tenth*," said David.

"That's possible," said Murray.

"Beatrice would like that, wouldn't she?" said David.

"Of course!" said Murray. "She'd love it!"

"How about the twenty-fifth?" said David.

"The twenty-fifth I could make by tomorrow," said Murray. He grabbed a broom and began to sweep up.

David went out the door. Behind him he could hear snipping, and then Murray began to sing.

.5.
NOBODY LIKES ME

"Happy Valentine's Day, Curtis," said Miriam.
"That's easy for you to say," said Curtis.
"What's the matter?" asked Miriam.
"Nothing much," said Curtis. "Just that nobody
 likes me, and I'll never get a valentine."

"Don't give up too soon," said Miriam.
She went away, but in a few minutes
she was back.
She handed Curtis a valentine.

"Thanks, Miriam," said Curtis.
He put the valentine in his shopping bag.
"I hope you feel better soon," said Miriam,
waving good-bye.
"I'll try," called Curtis, sniffing.

Avery came down the street. "Hi, Curtis,"
he said. "How's it going?"
"Okay," said Curtis.
"Did you get any valentines?" said Avery.
Curtis reached into his shopping bag
and pulled out a handful.
"Twelve so far," he said.

GUS

Everybody in the village liked Gus the tailor, and they all sent him valentines. Gus wished he could send a valentine back to each one, but he couldn't.

This year, Gus decided, things would be different. All year long he saved bits of red thread in the back of his shop.
By summer the thread made a ball half as tall as Gus himself, and by February the ball was higher than his head.

Late in the afternoon before Valentine's Day, when most people were home having their supper, Gus pushed the big ball of thread out the door of his shop and down the icy street, rolling it like a snowball.

The thread trailed behind him.

An hour later, when he finally got back to his shop, the ball was almost gone.

The next morning Gus opened his shop
as usual. The first customer was Veronica.
"Would you sew a button on this coat,
Gus?" she asked.
"Certainly, Veronica," said Gus.
"Oh, I almost forgot!" said Veronica.
"Today is Valentine's Day, isn't it?"
"I believe it is, Veronica," said Gus.
"Did you make any valentines?" asked
Veronica.
"One," said Gus. "Just one."

.7.
THE VALENTINE SHOW

In the late afternoon everybody in the village went to Sidney's barn to see the Valentine Show. They sat on piles of straw and watched the acts.

First there was the Sweetheart Ballet.

"What in the world is that supposed
to be?" said Clifford.
"It's a heart," said Vicky.
"Looks like two skunks and a fat bear
to me," said Clifford.

Then Lester came onstage.
"Now we're all going to sssing,"
he said. "All together now . . .
watch my tail . . .
one . . . two . . .

" 'Let me call you ssssweetheart. . . .' "

Everybody sang the song and clapped.
"Hooray for Lester!" they cried.
Lester bowed.

Next Clayton came onstage.
"Here's a special weather report," he said.
"A big cloud is headed our way. It doesn't
look like rain exactly, or snow, either.
It looks like . . . valentines!"

And a shower of valentines came floating down from the rafters, where Mona, Tina, and Mary Lou were dumping paper bags full of hearts. Everybody cheered.

Then Gus leaned over the railing at the top of the barn. "Don't go home just yet, please!" he called. "You're all invited to come up here for cookies, cider, and one last valentine!" Everybody went up the stairs. Gus gave them cider and passed the cookies.

"Delicious!" said Maureen.

"Not bad," said Murray.

"I don't see any valentine," said Clifford.
"You said we'd get a valentine, Gus."

"I almost forgot," said Gus.
 He put down the cookies. "I guess
 it's time for the valentine, everybody."
"Where is it?" said Beatrice.
"Yes—where?" said Miriam.

"Look out the windows!" said Gus.
Everybody crowded around the windows
and looked out.
At first they didn't see anything.
Then Tina cried, "I see a red thread!"
"I see it, too!" cried Mona.
Then everybody saw the one red thread
that was lying on the snow.

"It goes around the entire village!" said
 Clifford.
"It's in the shape of a heart!" said Mona.
"It's a valentine!" said Mary Lou. "A giant
 valentine for all of us!"
 Everybody clapped and cheered.
"Thank you, Gus!" they said. "Thank you!"
"Happy Valentine's Day," said Gus.

The End